CARTOON NETWORK™

SCOOBY-DOO

GHASTLY GIANT

BY JESSE LEON MCCANN

SCHOLASTIC INC.

New York Toronto London Auckland Sydney Mexico City New Delhi Hong Kong Buenos Aires

For Beth Dunfey — a wonderful editor and a joy to work with!

ISBN-13: 978-0-439-45523-7
ISBN-10: 0-439-45523-5

Cover design by Louise Bova
Interior design by Bethany Dixon

12 11   11 12/0

Printed in the U.S.A.   40

First printing, February 2003

Special thanks to Duendes del Sur for cover and interior illustrations.

Scooby-Doo and his friends were on their way to Craggy Mountain Camp. It was time for a vacation from solving mysteries! They were going to be camp counselors. The gang was looking forward to three weeks of fun and exploring with the kids who camped there.

"It says here that Craggy Mountain has more pits and drop-offs than any other mountain in the state," Velma read from the camp's brochure. "And the top of the mountain is almost always covered in a gloomy fog."

CRAGGY
MOUNTAIN
CAMP

2 MILES

"Like, I don't care if it has more craters than the moon, as long as the camp's kitchen is well stocked!" Shaggy licked his lips. "Right, Scoob?"

"Ruh-huh!" Scooby agreed.

As the gang piled out, they were met by the owner of the camp, Mr. Ross. Along with him came the other counselors. They were named Bruce, Benny, and Pauline.

4

"I am **so** glad you kids made it!" Mr. Ross smiled happily. "You're really going to bring home the bacon for me this year!"

"Racon?" Scooby's tummy started rumbling at the sound of that!

"Oh, look, guys!" said Benny. "The famous Mystery, Inc., kids are here! I guess we all know who will be the star counselors this summer."

"As if we didn't do a good enough job by ourselves last year," mumbled Pauline.

Mr. Ross asked Bruce, Benny, and Pauline to show Shaggy and Scooby where the camp's mess hall was. He knew they'd be hungry.

"It's going to be a prosperous season!" Mr. Ross said cheerily as he showed Fred, Velma, and Daphne to their cabins. "Having famous detectives like you as counselors really helped business – and I don't mind telling you, I love making money."

Fred, Daphne, and Velma looked at each other uncomfortably. They hadn't volunteered so Mr. Ross could make more money. They'd volunteered because they liked working with kids.

At the mess hall, the cook had prepared a huge, delicious meal for Shaggy and Scooby. They dug into it right away.

"Say, it's a good thing you guys are here," Bruce told them. "Maybe you can solve the mystery of the ghastly giant!"

"Yeah! It's big and hairy, and it tries to get you if you wander away from your friends," Pauline added in a spooky voice. "Or so the legend goes."

Honk! Honk!
"All right! The campers are here!" Benny said with a big smile.

Benny, Bruce, and Pauline ran out of the mess hall to greet the kids. Shaggy and Scooby followed, wondering about what the counselors had told them.

"Zoinks! Ghastly giant?" Shaggy gulped. "Did they mention it in the brochure?"

"Ri ron't rink ro!" Scooby answered shakily.

The kids were really delighted when they spotted Bruce, Benny, and Pauline. Many of the youngsters had been coming to the camp for years, so they were all old friends.

The kids were especially glad to see Scooby and the gang.

"Wow! Wait till my friends back home hear about Mystery, Inc., being here!" said one. "They'll want to come next year!"

"That's the idea! Tell all your friends." Mr. Ross grinned. "Why, with the money I'll make, I can retire a wealthy man!"

Suddenly, a huge, fancy limousine pulled up the dirt road toward the campground.

"Jackie's here!" hollered one of the girls, and a bunch of the campers went running up to say hello.

"It must be the little girl whose mom is Satin, the world-famous singing sensation," said Daphne. "Talk about arriving in style."

10

When the chauffeur opened the door, Satin appeared. "Oh, really, Jackie darling! I don't see why you insist on coming here year after year," she sniffed. "After all, now I can afford to send you to a much better camp."

"Don't be silly, Mom! There is no better camp than Craggy Mountain – all my friends are here!" Jackie exclaimed. She rushed out to greet the other campers.

That night, the campers huddled around the campfire in the cool mountain air. They sang songs and roasted hot dogs and marshmallows.

"It looks like Satin's not the only talented one in the family," Velma said, smiling. "Jackie can play a pretty mean guitar."

"Like, Scoob and I were so busy munching, we didn't even notice," Shaggy said between bites. "You're right, Velma. She's laying down some groovy tunes!"

"Roovy runes!" Scooby agreed, popping another marshmallow into his mouth.

Then, as the fire began to die down, it was time for spooky stories. Pauline told the scariest story that night. It was about the ghastly giant, and how it would hide in the fog and wait for an unsuspecting hiker to come along. She whispered about how, when a hiker would get near . . .

"**Rooowl!** I gotcha!" Bruce suddenly jumped out of the dark, wearing a scary mask. He gave everybody a fright – Scooby and Shaggy most of all!

Everyone laughed, but it seemed like Bruce, Benny, and Pauline were laughing at Scooby and Shaggy and how scared they were.

The next day, the camp counselors played another practical joke on Scooby-Doo and Shaggy. Pauline had told them to sit in a "place of honor." But when they did, a loose board flipped art supplies into the air. They were instantly covered with sticky glue and other stuff!

"Like, is it just me, or do the other counselors seem jealous that Mystery, Inc., is here this summer?" Shaggy asked Scooby.

"Ri ron't row." Scooby shrugged. It was hard for him to tell, since he was never jealous himself.

Later in the week, it was time for a big hike to the top of Craggy Mountain. Mr. Ross spent the whole hike trying to convince Jackie to talk her mother into giving a special benefit concert for the camp.

Benny spent the time teasing Shaggy and Scooby. He was telling them spooky stories about the giant. As everyone climbed higher and higher, it got foggier and foggier. And Shaggy and Scooby got more and more nervous!

Soon it was so foggy, it was hard to see everyone.

"You'll be okay if you stay on the path," Velma said loudly so they all could hear. "I think we're almost at the top!"

Suddenly, a huge figure appeared out of the mist. "**Aarrgh! Roowwwl!**"

"Zoinks!" cried Shaggy. "Like, it's the giant!"

"Roh, no!" Scooby-Doo backed away, motioning for the kids to follow him to safety.

Everybody scattered, and there was a lot of confusion. Velma was trying to keep the kids together when something bumped into her - hard.

"Oh, no! My glasses!" she cried.

The giant kept growling and picking up kids, looking at them, then putting them down again. It was very scary for the kids.

"Hey! Giant! Leave those kids alone!" Fred yelled.

All of a sudden, the giant spotted Jackie and ran straight toward her! "**Groowl! Huurgh!**"

At the same moment, Shaggy and Scooby backed right into a sticking, prickly bush. **Zoom!** They were so surprised, they leaped right into the giant.

"Good job, Shaggy and Scooby!" exclaimed Daphne. "That's the way to stop a big beastie!"

Daphne wanted to get Jackie back to the camp as soon as possible, so she ran downhill with Shaggy and Scooby. Unfortunately, the giant followed right behind them.

"Zoinks! Like, don't look now, Scoob, but we've still got company. Big, **ugly** company!" cried Shaggy.

"Reah! Rugly!" Scooby agreed.

"Jeepers! That creature sure seems interested in Jackie," Daphne said. "What's up with that?"

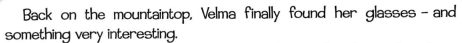

Back on the mountaintop, Velma finally found her glasses - and something very interesting.

"Jinkies! Satin's business card." Velma frowned. "What's this doing here?"

Velma got to her feet and looked around. No one was anywhere to be seen - not the giant, not the other counselors, not the kids. No one! Velma looked at Satin's card again. She was sure it was a clue.

Then she tucked it away and started running down the mountain trail.

With a little luck, Fred was able to get almost all the kids back to camp. He was worried because the rest of Mystery, Inc., the other counselors, Mr. Ross, and Jackie were all still missing. The cook said he hadn't seen anyone since they all left on the hike.

Fred looked around thoughtfully. His gaze stopped on some boxes nearby. They hadn't been there before. He was pretty sure he'd found a clue!

SKIT COSTUMES

SKIT COSTUMES

Meanwhile, things weren't going so well for Daphne. She was so worried about getting Jackie away from the giant, she didn't see one of the crevices until she was falling into it!

"Like, don't worry, Daph!" Shaggy cried. "Scooby and I will save you!"

"Rold ron, Raphne!" Scooby hollered. "Rold ron!"

"Don't worry about saving me, you guys!" Daphne yelled heroically. "That creature has snatched Jackie! Save her!"

Sure enough, the giant was running away, with Jackie under one arm.

"Help! Help!" Jackie cried.

Scooby and Shaggy knew it was important to save the little girl, but they couldn't leave Daphne in danger. Scooby quickly reached down his tail to Daphne. She grabbed it and was pulled to safety!

The giant kept running as fast as it could. The strange thing was, Jackie was almost positive she could hear it chuckling under its breath. "**Heh! Heh! Heh!**"

Luckily for Jackie, there was a surprise in store for that giant! Velma was hiding in the trees, with a branch pulled back tight. As soon as the giant got close enough, Velma let go of the branch.

Smack! The branch hit the giant square in the face!

The giant was so surprised, it let Jackie go. Velma was right there to scoop up the little girl and start running.

Velma and Jackie hid in a nearby cave. After the creature had passed, Velma told Jackie about finding her mother's card where the giant had first appeared.

"I wouldn't be surprised if my mom was behind this," Jackie said. "She didn't want me to come here this summer. She's probably trying to scare me into leaving. Everybody knows there's no such thing as real giants."

"If Fred were here, he'd want you to act as bait," Daphne said as she disguised Scooby and Shaggy. "Now, let's see if the giant is **only** interested in Jackie."

"Oh, man!" Shaggy grumbled. "Like, those mean old counselors are probably behind this giant thing. This is probably just another practical joke!"

"Reah!" Scooby sniffed in agreement. "Rean rold rounselors!"

Daphne, Shaggy, and Scooby-Doo didn't realize that someone was right behind them at that very moment. It was the giant!

"**Hoooowwrrl!**" The giant sounded **very** angry.

"Zoinks!" Shaggy cried. "On second thought, maybe it is a real giant! What if it ate Jackie and now wants more kids?! Like, run!"

"Roh, no! Relp! Relp!" Scooby yelled.

Daphne, Shaggy, and Scooby weren't the only ones who got a big fright. When they ran into the other counselors hiding behind some bushes, there was plenty of panic all around!

Bruce was so frightened, he started shaking. Benny was shivering. Pauline was quaking. They joined Scooby, Shaggy, and Daphne and ran as fast as they could away from the charging, howling giant.

"Gosh!" cried Pauline. "Is it like this for you guys all the time?"

"Like, pretty much," Shaggy replied, running at full speed. "Sometimes we get weekends off!"

Just as the creature got within grabbing distance, Shaggy and Scooby hid behind some trees and stuck their feet out. The giant was caught off-guard. He tripped and went flying!

Benny was really impressed. "W-wow, guys! That was some pretty fast thinking! Thanks!"

"Ron't rention rit," Scooby said modestly.

Unfortunately, the giant flew into the cave where Velma and Jackie were hiding.

"Jinkies! Look out!" cried Velma.

Before anyone knew what had happened, the creature had grabbed Jackie again. "**Growwwl!**" it howled with delight.

But the giant didn't get very far. Fred had left the other campers with the cook and come back just in time to snare the giant!

"Now, let's see just who this giant really is!" Fred began to pull off the creature's mask.

"I'll bet it's my mom's chauffeur!" Jackie said.

"Ri'll ret rit's rose rean rold rounselors . . ." Scooby looked suddenly at Bruce, Benny, and Pauline. "Roh. Rever rind."

"Nope!" Velma smiled. "It's . . ."

"Mr. Ross!" Velma declared.

"I used the camp's skit costumes to dress up like the giant. I was going to kidnap Jackie and get her rich mother to pay a lot of ransom money," Mr. Ross grumbled. "And I would have gotten away with it, too, if . . ."

"We know! 'If it wasn't for us meddling kids and our dog!'" The Mystery, Inc., gang laughed.

The counselors were really grateful to Shaggy and Scooby for saving them. They apologized for being so mean to them before. Pauline even gave Scooby-Doo a big kiss.

"Raw, rucks!" Scooby blushed.

When Jackie's mom found out about the whole thing, she decided to buy Craggy Mountain Camp. The camp wouldn't have to close down and Jackie could keep coming there with her friends.

Satin even joined Jackie at the camp for the rest of her stay. All in all, it was a pretty fine camping experience, thanks to some first-class mystery solving – and a dog named Scooby-Doo.